To: Tiana From U.M
Love you.

You Can't Sit

With Us!

T. E. Williams

T. E. WILLIAMS

This Book Is Dedicated To Boom Kini

T. E. WILLIAMS

Special Thanks To

Walter Gleaton and Sabrina Shelton

T. E. WILLIAMS

Chapter 1 – "Mommy Don't Play"

Simone Moncrieff came running down Edgewood Avenue to the front door of her home with an angry mob of 10 year olds marching behind her instigating and taunting, acting as rowdy as teens at a basketball game. Her mother stood on the porch with one hand on her hip, the other holding onto an unlit cigarette. She didn't make a move until she knew for sure Simone wasn't in any real danger.

These girls out here like to jump people and if it was going down like that, Ms. Joyce would *not* have dialed 911, she would have gone down there to fight side by side with her daughter. When she saw the tough looking tomboy stop in the middle of the sidewalk throwing her backpack to the ground she knew it was going to be a one on one fight.

Simone's heart was pounding 90mph. The boys in the crowd made matters much worse wanting to see them fight. They'd been hearing the rumors spread throughout the day, especially during lunch, how it was going down after school. Aurora Trotter threatened to 'kick her butt' since gym class just before lunch, and the lunch monitors and crossing guards were on high alert in case anything popped off on school property.

When she finally reached the next door neighbor's tree, feeling like she was one step away from a port in the storm, Ms. Joyce turned, opened her heavy metal screen door, went through it; then locked it! She lit the cigarette then blew a billow of smoke through the screen holding on to the latch. "Momma, open the door! Let me in!" Simone protested! Ms. Joyce shook her head, "No Mony, go handle what you need to handle! I'll be right here! Go'on! Go take care of your business, or you'll be running forever!"

Simone feeling the gulp in her throat but not able to swallow turned to face the loud, rowdy mob with water in her eyes. Turning quickly back around to her only refuge, she pleads,

"Mommy, please! I don't want to fight!" She begs with enormous sorrowful eyes, but her pleas fell onto deaf ears. "Simone Moncrieff! Take that jacket off walk down there and get it done!"

Simone must've felt a thousand bricks in her shoes and in her 10 year old heart, but she knew her mother was not playing. She stood with her shoulders tightened, stiff and rigid, her spine hot with fear. Hearing the sound of her own heartbeat, the boys chanting and her mother's last words, she turned and walked slowly down the walk to where Aurora stood on the sidewalk pushing her sleeves up, head tilted, putting on a good show preparing to tear her head off. Ms. Joyce took another puff of her cigarette and tossed her hair back leaning against the door jamb, "Get it done Simone, before the sirens!"

The girl takes a swing and hits Simone square on the chin then follows with a left to her cheek but Simone had never been hit in the face before and when the second blow connected, Simone threw up her hands, planted her feet, stooped low and punched Aurora with a combination of blows Laila Ali would have to give her props for! After, Aurora Trotter couldn't hear, but she could see the crowd belted over in laughter with their hands over their mouths. When the buzz went away and her hearing returned she realized she was still being hit!

Simone was bent over her banging her head against the curb and it took 3 boys to pull her away. Aurora, whose eye was purple and swollen shut had blood gushing out from her temple and her top lip! She never knew what hit her.

The fight wasn't a fight. It was a beat down; brought on by Simone's fear of who she thought was the duke of the school. Getting hit in the face had enraged her. One boy lifted Simone's hand high into the air, while Aurora's friends helped her up off the ground tending to her wounds and wiping the dirt off her clothes. The boys were giggling and making jokes while Aurora ran away humiliated.

Simone still standing motionless breathing heavily with her fists still balled up was snapped out of her rage by the sound of the sirens one street over. She picked up her back pack and walked into the house where Ms. Joyce held the door open to let her only daughter in. "Now go wash up" Ms. Joyce said quietly putting the cigarette out.

Through the years after the notorious 5th Grade fight Simone and Aurora established their own cliques who were loyal to them but with each other they were always bumping heads. They were in many school social clubs together and seemed to have the same interests; Student Government, Color Guards, Yearbook Staff, Future Business Leaders Club and they both were in endless talents shows. Always giving each other a hard time and gossiping about one another. They even liked the same boys.

Simone's reputation preceded her since the old days so she never had to fight again, but she certainly did her part to maintain her standing by learning to talk tough to keep the wolves away. When ever someone new came to the school, they were told that she's not the one to play around with. In the city, the tougher you appear, the more dangerous you seem to newcomers. Simone's face was usually expressionless so she didn't exactly come off as approachable. Grown people said she looked mean. She was the girl whose nose sweat was visible even when it wasn't hot out. She walked hard too. Ms. Joyce complained every time she thundered down the steps.

Simone wasn't the type of person to start trouble but she could handle it if it came her way. Her peers would go out of their way to keep her as an ally. She really didn't have to persuade anyone of anything. Teachers were leery of her because she could shoot you a look that would make you rethink speaking to her in a certain way. And if she ever rolled her eyes, let's just say you know you mucked up.

At home she and her mother shared a close, deep relationship and Simone felt she could talk to her about anything. Her mother had set up a college fund for her the last couple of months while Simone prepared herself scholastically for college, taking SATs and applying to several universities. Ironically, she was interested in Theology, but Simone was the neighborhood hair stylist also. She did hair to put some cash in her pocket.

Aurora Trotter had an older brother and a younger sister. She was working an after school job at Foot Locker to assist the family and save enough for her classes in August. She intended to pay credit by credit at the Community College until she earned her Associates Degree. Their father was in their lives but did not live in the home. Their mother worked as a Dental Assistant at an office in Ewing. She worked long hours and Aurora was responsible for cleaning and cooking for them.

Aurora's brother who also works for Foot Locker graduated the year prior. Barbara Trotter was becoming increasingly concerned about his friends and the tempting drug trade which can look quite glamorous to young people so she made him get a job too. The neighborhood they lived in was one you locked the door as you drove through.

Chuck was happy to be working and getting discounts on Nike gear. Aurora was a saver, and what she didn't save went into the household, but her brother spent his entire check every week. Occasionally, he'd take their little sister Connie on a mini shopping spree.

Aurora had learned to shop at thrift stores and consignment shops. She had her own style; she didn't follow trends too often and most of the time, she could be seen in the black and white referee uniform given to her by her employer. Whatever shift she got were the hours that her brother didn't so one could be home with Connie. Even though Chuck was hired because of Aurora, he got more hours than she did. He was well liked on the job, too. When their supervisor made the schedule it favored Chuck.

Chapter 2 – "Senior Cut Day"

It was Senior Cut Day, and the entire Senior Class drove whatever they could get their hands on to get to Washington Crossing Park to celebrate. People brought charcoal and coolers, balls of every sort, and the music! The teens bought wine coolers and weed, being that the group was unsupervised. They were considered young adults and were representative of that group just happy to close the high school chapter and ready for their next challenges.

For Aurora, this was a vacation day from work. She had no intentions of dealing with smelly feet and rude customers at Foot Locker, and welcomed what was supposed to be a day of leisure. Her crew, Ursula, Casey and Sage were under a shady tree waiting for the hamburgers and hot dogs, throwing back fruited wine coolers and talking about guys. Sage was the one who started it up and the others just agreed to agitate the situation. "Simone got on them tight ass jean shorts, she gone give herself a yeast infection!" she said. That's all it took for Aurora, who had on similar jean shorts to laugh loudly as Simone walked by. Aurora rolled her eyes, "She do that shit on purpose, she know she got too much ass for them shorts!" All the girls chimed in unison, "mmhm".

The rising sound of Aurora's laughter caused Simone to naturally look over to where the girls were huddled ear to ear in the lined up beach chairs. Of course, Simone rolled her eyes at the entire group. She continued to walk pass them to where the boys were setting up the horseshoes. "I'm in!" She hollered out to one of them picking up a horseshoe. She wore her blonde hair in a pony tail for the festivities and a red tank top with the jean shorts.

Aurora threw back what remained in the bottle and told Sage to go over to the ice cooler to get her another. Sage was more than happy to do whatever for Aurora and jumped to the task. In the interim, Casey began taking one cornrow out of her hair and asked Ursula to start unraveling on the other side. "Why you taking your hair out?" asked Aurora twisting up her face, "This ain't the place for that!" Ursula immediately dropped the braid and started cleaning her nails. "I'm combining these braids if you must know!" Casey had a good length of hair which was thick and it took hours for her to put her braids in. They were all braided back off her brown face and the style she wore was appropriate for the outing.

Sage returned with the wine cooler for Aurora who popped it open and took a long sip. Sage immediately goes over and helps unravel the braid on Casey's head that Ursula neglected to finish. Aurora looks at all of them and says, "I don't let everybody in MY hair". Casey dropped her hands and looks at Aurora "What the hell is your drama today, dang-ah? Ya' ass should've gone to work if you can't relax!"

Aurora and Casey always talked to each other as if they weren't friends, but the fact is Casey was one of Aurora's oldest because she was there picking Aurora up off the ground back in the day after Simone decked her. So she always kept that ammunition in the back of her mind.

She'd be quick to remind Aurora too. Ursula was a newcomer and she was just happy to have any friends. Sage and Ursula were followers, and didn't really have a solid reason to ridicule or demean Simone. They were just along for the ride. Aurora had always surrounded herself with people she could run. It made her feel like she was a leader, yet deep down, Aurora was kind of a follower herself. She needed them so she could always have information on Simone.

"I'm just saying" Aurora defended her statement even though she really didn't have an answer for Casey. Sage continued to unravel the braid she was on, "Your hair looks cute today Aurora." She had it cut short into a bob that came across the earlobes. Aurora wore the same style most days so the statement Sage offered was moot. Casey stuck out ducky lips at Aurora as if to say "Suck Up". Aurora stuck her tongue out at her.

Sage finished combining the two braids for Casey then sat back down in the beach chair next to Aurora. A familiar song came on that the crew recognized immediately. They jump up into formation and the four of them start to perform an organized Sorority style dance which draws attention from the other Seniors who crowd around cheering for them.

Simone Moncrieff stops playing horseshoes and Dizzy, Simone's best friend looks over at Aurora and her friends, "They kill me! They just can't do anything on their own. They always got to line up like a bunch of robots! Look at Aurora with them tight ass shorts on!" Simone replied, "What'd you expect? It's Senior Cut Day."

One of the guys on the grill announced that the food was ready, "Y'all line up!" he yells and Simone and Dizzy head for the grill to start the line. The concessions were displayed on picnic tables on the concrete platform which was in the center of the park. Tables were under a large pavilion where folks were already going over to sit. Simone stood in line after grabbing her utensils, "Dizzy what you want? I'll get your plate just go get us a table. I don't want to be nowhere near *Vader*!" Referring to Aurora, a pet name she gave her back in the 7th Grade.

Dizzy responded, "I just want a hamburger and baked beans, oh and get me some potato salad." Then she takes off to find a suitable table for the two of them and Simone's cousin Papillion

Toussaint, nicknamed Poppy, who was one of the guys monitoring the mountainous bouncy bounce the teens used to jump into the lake. He'd be along soon.

When Simone comes over with the plates the song Aurora and her crew was dancing to ended and they all walked behind her, snickering and trying to get a rise out of her. Simone didn't break stride but her *Spidey Sense* was tingling. She didn't trust them and stayed on high alert whenever they were in her vicinity.

Simone's jaw tightened. Dizzy stood in preparation just in case anything was going down. Poppy must've also felt the vibe because he began his descent from the hill of the area of the bouncy bounce to the pavilion. "Everything copacetic, Simone?" Simone hollered out, "Yeah, I'm good over here" lifting her leg over the bench to sit, as Poppy continued to walk toward her with a concerned look. They sat down with Dizzy who dug into the chow. Dizzy said, "Them hoes ain't got no chill!" Simone wasn't bothered at all and gave it no more thought than shooing a fly away.

Poppy always looked out for Simone. He had been left back from the year before so had to do his twelfth grade over again. Some say he did it on purpose to graduate with her. Simone and Poppy had to attend a funeral in Haiti last year for their Grandfather. Poppy stayed longer and the Trenton School System penalized him for it. He had missed too many days and had to repeat.

Poppy was a handsome guy, short very dark pretty skin and very muscular. His forearms were wide like Popeye's and his walk, like Simone's gait, could be quite intimidating. He still held his accent, and he would do anything to protect her; not that she needed it.

Dizzy took a scoop of the baked beans and shoved it into her mouth. Simone not engaging in the conversation that Dizzy began sat quietly eating her ribs when Poppy got up to get his plate in the long line that formed. He passed by the table where Aurora sat and overheard them talking about Simone on the return trip. "They over there yapping about you like it's nothing else to talk about" he said, "I mean really it's time to grow up!"

Simone kept eating. "You know she don't want it with me Cousin. She's just all talk, found that out long time ago." Just then, the Class President Terrell Jacobs began the welcome speech to the class on the microphone. The speakers were set up all over the park. Terrell pointedly reminded everybody to be responsible, to clean up behind themselves and to have a good time. Everybody returned to their food and when they finished, they went back to all the games that were set up for the affair. Besides horseshoes and the bouncy bounce there was a bull ride, a boxing ring for Sumo wrestling, the three legged race, an obstacle course, tug of war, and water balloon fight set up.

Simone decided she was done with the horseshoe game and she and Dizzy went over to the three legged race. Aurora and her crew followed everything Simone did throughout the event to try to intimidate her. It was as if they were intentionally trying to pursue her with the purpose of nothing good. Simone told Poppy to stay close because she just knew in this forum it wouldn't be a surprise if something did pop off.

Terrell Jacobs and Quay Livingston suited up for the Sumo wrestling match. All the spectators stood 'round chanting for each competitor laughing about how they looked in the comical looking inflatable outfits! The match was even. Carter hit the gong with the mallet and the two face off! They were quite entertaining bumping each other's bellies and flopping all over the place! Many spectators were using their cell phones to video the spectacle.

Simone acted like she was a corner man and helped Terrell by rubbing his fake shoulders in the first round. They met in the middle again and Carter hit the gong. They were at it again! Simone shouted, "Livingston is down! Livingston is down!" When Terrell pinned Quay down rolling all over top of him! It was hilarious!

Carter jumped inside the ring and hung a fake award around Terrell's neck raising his hand. Terrell put his foot on Quay's big belly then assumed the quintessential Sumo stance flexing his fake muscles and shaking his head from side to side! "Who's next? Who's next?" He shouted like a warrior! That's when Quay got up and said, "Let the girls go! It's the girls turn!" Simone was the first to volunteer. She was having a great time and it did look awfully fun. She said, "It's go time, suit me up! Suit me up!" Terrell taking off the suit asked for another female volunteer, "Anyone? Anybody want to go?"

Now was Aurora's shining moment. She squeezes through the crowd with her arm in the air. As soon as Simone heard her voice and saw Aurora's signature dangling Yin/Yang bracelet raised she knew it was her. Simone flexes her jaw and throws her head from side to side waiting to be zipped up. "No problem! Let's get this done!" The crowd went crazy, knowing the history of the two they were waiting in anticipation on the edge of their seats. The guys started placing bets and the girls came closer to the ring, cell phones at the ready.

Sage gets to the corner before Aurora and starts announcing her arrival, "Trotter you got this, Trotter! Ain't nobody scurd!" She yelled antagonizing and instigating. Dizzy looks eye to eye with Simone and they press their foreheads together, "Whoop her ass Mony!" Simone let's out a rebel yell and they meet in the middle of the ring. Terrell gets between the two covering the microphone, "Are you guys sure you want to do this, you know everybody expects you fight *for real*, right?" Simone sticks her ducky lips out, "It is what it is, yo, it's whatever!" So, hearing her response, Aurora bending low like a real Sumo wrestler, "We ain't in Elementary no more, I'm about to smash this chick!"

The gong couldn't sound quickly enough! The minute it was sounded, Terrell backs out of the ropes and they were off. Both girls were around the same height, 5' 7" and around the same weight class. Simone had a little more meat on her than Aurora. The crowd of spectators is going crazy shouting out each bang of the bellies. Carter stood by making sure they followed the rules. They weren't doing any significant damage in the first round, but that didn't matter. They were finally eye to eye expressing what they each felt without words.

They had an intense hate between them and if sparks could be seen it would have been a spectacular array of sight and sound like the Fourth of July! All of a sudden, like Déjà Vu,

Aurora takes a swing at her! Simone shouted, "Sucker punch? Really?" then she counters with a combination and it's on! They are fighting and pulling each other's hair! Simone frees her hair and head buts Aurora and she goes down! Aurora, looking like a turtle on its back squirming around the mat is trying her best to get up in this inflatable costume which is awkward and cumbersome. Simone dives down and starts to pummel Aurora but Terrell who expected the whole scene pulls Simone off and raises her hand in the air. "Winner" he says shaking his head. Dizzy looked at Simone and mouthed the words, "Two for two" flashing the peace sign twice.

Chapter 3 – "When Push Comes To Shove"

Looking out at the rain Simone took a breather from studying for her final exams, stretching like a cat. She walked down the hall to her mother's room where Mrs. Joyce Moncrieff is kneeling in prayer. She slightly opened the door to her room and shut it again, but her mom called her back, "Come on in Mony, I'm done." Simone flopped down on her bed and her mom reached for her head to place it in her own lap.

She swiped her hand across Simone's hairline. Simone welcomed her touch, the most soothing and calming of touches. Only a mother could touch you in such a way that the world literally goes away and the comfort of home within you comes forth to reveal all vulnerabilities and shame. She and her mother knew she could release all the tension in her life with one touch from her mother. They'd only had each other.

Joyce began to hum, *I Need Thee*, an old Gospel hymn that always comforted the both of them. Simone kept her eyes closed and listened to the rhythm of her heartbeat along with the hum. She began to hum too. Then, when the sound of the rain and the tenderness of the moment, they both began to sing aloud, *"'Every Hour, I Need Thee..."* The rain and the two of them in harmony was a blend of Alto and Soprano that compared sweetly, like dueling banjos in sync and in tune, as if entertaining the angels that were surrounding them. And the smell of lilac from the pretty vase of flowers that she had picked for her mother that afternoon before the rain.

No more needed to be done or said. Just the bond of the quiet duo tied together in a flow of elegance and whispers, *"Oh bless me now my Savior, I Come To Thee, I Need Thee Oh...I Need Thee..."* Simone dozed off in her mother's lap after the last verse. But her mother continued with the tune, raising her hands in the air to praise the Lord, thanking Him for her child who had overcome so many obstacles no one knew of. The many sacrifices she had made for Simone and the rage only He can calm because she knew she had passed it on to her daughter. She had become passive now in her late 40's and was still quite beautiful. She loved her daughter with tremendous humility. Simone had been conceived through true Agape love and not run of the mill lust. She was born in one of the most horrible blizzards in the history of New Jersey leaving 30-inches of snow on the ground while Joyce lay in the hospital with a permanent smile under her belly where the doctor had performed an emergency C-Section.

She was not able to hold her dear sweet baby the entire seven day stay. Simone Moncrieff was born with strawberry splotches all over her body and had long blond hair which came down over into her face making it considerably difficult to distinguish her hairline which continued right to her eyebrows. She was a beautiful baby, 6lbs 12oz, 21 inches. Joyce's mother admitted Simone would be a force to reckon with, being born in a blizzard. Truer words have not been said.

At 19, Joyce's tiny birth canal could not accommodate her size and after 7 hours it had been decided that further dilation could cause distress for this baby. When she was finally able to see the baby she wanted to give her a name that meant strength. They warned her that because she had general anesthesia, the baby would be lethargic; Joyce had to sign papers before they wheeled her into the OR. Her husband William was holding the baby as she opened her eyes and as Joyce went to reach for her, she felt the unbearable pain in her body, even though she was numbed.

He leaned in with her so that Joyce could look at the bundle all wrapped up in a pink blanket. Simone was so small in it, and she also had a pinkish hue, so it was hard to see exactly where in the blanket she was if not for the strawberry splotches all over her little face. When she grabbed her tiny hand she yawned and stretched like a cat in the blanket pushing it off of herself then opened her eyes as if to say "I've arrived!" William said it was her 'Red Carpet' moment.

He called her a princess, but Joyce corrected him. She said, "This baby will be no princess. Simone is going to be a fighter. Against all odds, she will come up against some of the toughest opponents and prevail!" All her life Simone had proven to be one of the toughest people Joyce had ever known. She had such a rage within her when faced with confrontation. She didn't at first understand the rage and would turn away. But in her 18 years, the more someone came at her, the more enraged she became. She never backed down or ran away from it nor gave her opponent credit unless she deserved it.

Only Joyce truly understood.

T. E. WILLIAMS

Chapter 4 – "It's Not Fair"

Poppy came over picking in the stew Joyce made that had rested on the stove to cool. Simone called out to him. "Poppy! Get out of Mommy's stew!" Poppy dropped the spoon and looked around wondering where the damn cameras were. "How does she do that...??!" He whispered to himself. "How'd you know I was here Mony?" He yelled back, reaching for a hunk of bread and a bowl.

Simone came downstairs in her pink bathrobe and bunny slippers. "I know every sound of this house, you know that." Poppy picked her up and swung her around "What's up chick?" then began to ladle the soup out of the pot. He made a bowl for her and then a bowl for himself. Dipping the hunk of bread in the stew Poppy says to her, "All ready for finals?" Simone pulls two spoons out of the drawer and tosses one to

Poppy. "I finished all my finals, I'm just waiting for the grades, how 'bout you?" With a mouthful of bread Poppy is still trying to spoon more stew into his mouth, "I'm through too, I did alright too." She looks up, "How do you know?" Simone knew the grades hadn't been posted yet. "I cheated off you!" He admits! "So stupid!" She says and takes an air swipe at him.

After the meal they sat in the den watching and laughing at the comedy show on television when came an unusual knock at the door. Simone asked, "Who is it?" Poppy being closer to it was the one who got up to open it, and as soon as he did, he was shot in the chest by the mysterious person in all black who ran off! Simone screamed, "Oh my God!" then chased the perpetrator through the neighbor's driveway where he leaped over a back fence.

She ran back grabbed her phone and dialed 911 while trying to attend to Poppy who was already gone. She screamed for help and dropped the phone. Joyce was not at home. She went to a night service at church where she was expected to usher for the evening. When she returned, her house was surrounded by police and ambulances.

She attempted to run into the house, "Simone, Where's my Mony?" She screamed at detectives who assured her that she was okay, "Unfortunately your nephew Papillion Toussaint has been murdered, ma'am. Your daughter identified him and his folks have been called." Joyce doubled over "Oh no! Where's Mony?" She yelled for her, "Simone!" She came running out still in the bathrobe and slippers.

They hugged for a moment and Simone told her how he answered the door to a gunshot blast. Poppy wasn't into anything criminal so the detectives asked, "Who else lives in the home?" to which Simone answered, "No one but me and mommy!" It led the detectives to believe that one of them may have been the target, but they didn't speak it.

Simone and Joyce sat on the stoop wondering together who would shoot somebody at the front door. It didn't make any sense. "We are peaceful people, and Simone is only in high school and so is Poppy! He don't mess with nobody! It's so unfair!" Joyce volunteers.

"Ma'am" the detective said to Simone, "Do you have a description of the person who killed Poppy? Did you see anything?" He asked. "I chased that fool through the alley and he jumped over the fence! I had to get back to call 911!" Simone admitted. "We'd like to have a formal statement from you at the station, if that's okay." The other stated. "Let me put some clothes on." She said as Poppy's mother Sarah, Joyce's sister came upon the scene. They hadn't even taken Poppy's body away yet. All the neighbors were outside. It was such a sad scene.

Joyce was surprised that Simone was taking it as well as she was, but the truth is it hadn't sunk in yet. That night, the traumatic event was manifested in nightmare after nightmare; the sound of the gun going off and the way Poppy fell to the floor, a sight and a sound she will never forget.

Joyce had to come in and put cool compresses on Simone's head and sat with her most of the night. She ran back and forth between Sarah and Simone tending to them. Everything was as if it would never be discovered who did this or why. Simone sat up to read her Bible and the tears just kept coming. She loved her cousin and now he was gone. It had occurred to her that he was doing all he could to graduate from high school and the thought that he wouldn't caused her to cry even harder. She thought of his mother Sarah and how proud she would have been to see him walk down the aisle to receive his diploma.

The thought caused Simone to cry so tenderly holding her Bible consumed by grief. She felt so utterly helpless, but began to pray. In her deep prayer and concentration, she kept seeing Poppy's face, so handsome and strong, always by her side and making her laugh. The last moments he spoke with the stew and bread making his cheek bulge. You just never know when God is going to call you home.

She decided that night in honor of him she'd finish high school and enroll at seminary for Theology/Religious Studies. She had always known she wanted to celebrate with Papillion planning in her head how they'd throw an impromptu graduation party, but now that plan is out. They graduate in a couple of weeks. "God whatever your plan is for my life, I will honor you. I'm heartbroken! Please help me get through this Father!"

At the funeral, the two sisters sat next to each other and clung to each other and Simone was feeling a bit outcast, but she understood. They had been pregnant together with them and they were their only children. She realized that she had to be strong for the two ladies; no one should have to bury a child. Simone took the reigns with some of the funeral arrangements and the repast. She had had her cry. When they got out to the cemetery, Simone was one of the few people who stood to speak after the pastor asked if anyone had wanted to say something.

Simone spoke of how they grew up together side by side. She talked about how protective he was; the closeness, more like brother and sister, and how they made the trip together to Haiti last year to say goodbye to their grandfather, yet Papillion decided to stay to help out, sacrificing his Senior Year. How heavy her heart felt because of his loss, and added, "I will honor my cousin by starting Theologian School in the fall. If anybody has any information about who may have murdered him, any information that could help, please come forward." She could not finish. Other mourners had to catch her because she fainted.

T. E. WILLIAMS

Chapter 5 – "A Ray of Hope"

Aurora Trotter sat at the lunch table with the usual suspects, Ursula, Casey and Sage. Dizzy was out that day and Simone was feeling especially lonesome and forlorn. She got her tray with a slice of pizza and a cup of peaches. People were approaching her saying sentiments of sympathy and wishing her well.

She walked over by the table where they sat not realizing she was no longer in safe territory, Sage boldly stood, but Aurora grabbed her arm and she sat back down. Simone looked over at Aurora with no expression on her face nodding ever so slightly then continued to walk over to a vacant table. She began to cry and tears were falling into the peach cup. Many people came over to comfort her. She could not finish the day and signed herself out.

When she got home she sat on her bed and had a good cry to get it all out of her system. She missed Poppy and was still wondering what had happened. She picked up the phone to call the detective she talked to at the station. He had given her his card. She dialed the number, "Yes, this is Simone Moncrieff, Papillion Toussaint's cousin, have you any information on who killed him yet?" The cop sounded as if he was caught off guard, "Simone? Yes, Simone" digging through files on his desk.

"Hello? Simone asked. "Yes Simone, if you can come down to the station I'd like to update you on what we have so far". He said. "I'm on my way!" Simone answered, and was on her way.

Simone got down to the Police Station and asked for Det. Hadley who was handling Poppy's case. He sat with her on a bench asking her to detail once more the description she gave of the perpetrator. "6' 2", wearing all black, very agile, he got up over that fence like it wasn't even a barrier. I had on slippers, big ones, and was not able to keep up with him." She said. "It has come to our attention through our investigation Simone that you do have some enemies. You haven't been honest with us." He said. Simone began to feel the rage coming up from her chest. "I don't have any enemies, not enemies that would kill!" she yelled, "Apparently some of your school mates disagree. Do you know Aurora Trotter?" Her expression changed, "Oh, yeah, we both are graduating Thursday. We're not really..." Det. Hadley interrupted, "Simone, are you aware that she has a brother who was on the basketball team?" Simone's eyes were working like an accountant's calculator. "Yeah, Chuck. He graduated last year". The detective said, "Could it have been him?"

Simone leaned back against the bench. "I don't know. I couldn't see his face! I...I'm not sure!" She stuttered. "Listen, he fits the description you gave and we're calling him down for a line up. Simone, do you remember his feet as he glided up the fence? Try to remember, it's important". She closed her eyes and envisioned the guy scaling the fence. His legs were long. She pictured Chuck doing a lay up. The picture became clear to her. "He had on black New Balances, um...maybe size...11? But Aurora and I aren't out to kill each other I..."

"Let me explain something to you. The way it was told to me at the school, after you decked Aurora Senior Cut Day there wasn't a lot of rebound from it." He said. "Well it just sort of died down, I guess Sir..." The cop looked at the innocence being displayed; or was it naivety? "Simone, you humiliated that girl! Twice! That's not something that just dies down. All your classmates said she always tries to join the clubs you join, likes the same boys as you; I mean she even has a tattoo that reads 'Vengeance is Mine'! Did you know that their mother took Chuck down South? Coincidence? I think not! Poppy is your cousin, and he would have done anything for you. He would do anything to protect you, right?"

Now the wheels are turning full speed in Simone's head. "This is crazy! I can see Chuck doing a layup in my mind...it's possible." The thought captivated her. Then logic came back and she wouldn't accept it, "Aurora's brother would kill Poppy over something I did to her? It just doesn't add up!" The cop waits a second for Simone, not of limited intelligence but maybe still in denial, to catch up. He offers, "No Simone, you were the one who was supposed to open that door, remember? Now think about it! In your statement, you said Poppy popped up unexpectedly, so he wasn't supposed to be there; ordinarily he would *not* have been the one to open the door. You also said as soon as it was opened, the gunfire rang out.

Now, you have to remember, this is what I do for a living. Does your mother go to service the same night each week?" He said flipping through his note pad. "Oh my God! Oh my God!" Simone exclaimed. Detective Hadley tilted his head to the side and grabbed her hand. The rage inside her turned to guilt, and she burst into tears, her hand over her mouth.

He continued, "How has Aurora been treating you lately?" Simone thought about the earlier in the lunch room where Sage stood with the '*You can't sit with us*' body language. The 2-second eye contact she made with Aurora, thinking it was a 'let her live, she just lost her cousin' look. That may have been guilt over knowing what her brother did. Simone was uncomfortably enlightened.

Detective Hadley received a call on his cell phone. "Yeah, she's here with us now. Okay on my way…" and hangs up. "Chuck has been picked up in Atlanta. He's being extradited back here in connection with this. Make yourself available because we're putting him in a lineup.

Now, don't set on your mind on the fact that it *was* him. It may have been. We're going to ask each suspect to do a layup so you can see the flow and fluidity of his leg movements. It's not 100% that it's him. Don't use it just because I planted that seed. I want you to really, really look. I want to get this guy off the street." Simone tried to compose herself. "Who else got motive? We don't have no drugs or money? Besides, it wasn't like it was a home invasion; He just blasted!" He looked at her, "We'll get to the bottom of it. Trust me." She nodded still feeling numb.

Chapter 6 – "The Line Up"

Simone came back for the lineup with her mother Joyce. Her eyes were swollen and red from all the crying in the past week. They stood in a little room, like you see on television with the huge one-way window. She paced and rubbed her head. Her mother moved a little closer to her and took hold of her hand, "I'm here baby" she whispered.

The screen opened and the first guy came running in. He was around 6-feet tall and had a very stylish layup but you could clearly see he wasn't trying to be fancy. It was his real layup. This was not the guy. Then the next guy came up but his feet immediately disqualified him. He was tall, 6' 2", but his feet were super long, easily a 13. Simone shook her head.

Then it happened. The third came in. It was Aurora's brother. Simone looked at his feet. He didn't even have to do the layup. She recognized the scuff on the New Balance! Dumb ass wore the same shoes he did the night of the shooting! It really was him, and that really was the reason! When she came to the realization she allowed him to do the layup before she spoke. She knew right away, it was Chuck. Chuck tried to kill her. The layup only confirmed what the scuff mark and her heart told her. He was really smooth with it like his leg didn't go up until the last possible moment. That hesitation, that's what did it for her. "That's him" she said without question, "That's who shot Poppy."

Simone and Joyce walked out of the room feeling confident he would be tried and convicted because of her identification. "Aurora knew Ma. You think someone could be that hateful and vengeful?" She asked. Joyce put her arm around her, "I have seen people kill over 2 quarters Mony. Hell, get it out your head that people need a reason at all." With that, Simone thought of how her mother would be if she had answered the door instead of Poppy. A .38 caliber bullet lodged into her heart. Again, she got emotional and cried thanking God for sparing her life, yet missing her cousin. "I think the purpose for his life was to be there to protect me." She said. "Well, he did his job then, didn't he?" Your cousin was a good man. I know because I helped raise him."

Chuck Trotter was booked on a Capital Murder charge and sent away obtaining the services of a Public Defender. It was all based on her testimony and the flight to Atlanta. How was Simone going to get through graduation or the rest of the week for that matter looking into Aurora's eyes?

It was hard enough grieving and living with the knowledge that it could have been her; should have been her. Survivor's guilt can be just as bad as what Aurora is dealing with. She did consider the fact that what Chuck had in his head didn't necessarily mean that Aurora wanted death. Maybe he was just supposed to scare the crap out of her. Then she thought about what Detective Hadley said after speaking to her classmates, her being jealous, and being humiliated. Her mother's words about not needing a reason; was that enough?

Aurora was upward bound. She wouldn't put her future or Chuck's future in jeopardy. Why would he even have a gun? He was working at

Foot Locker, living where he could live rent free, helping taking care of his little sister. It all was senseless. Especially since graduation is so close and she would be out of Aurora's life forever. Yes, she confirmed that it was him, and yes he *was* protective of Aurora. Why go to the degree of murder? His mother raised all of them. As hateful as she is, she couldn't have known about his plan. Simone had gone back and forth with it 100 times. Then she decided she would walk right up to Aurora and ask, come what may.

Aurora was in line in the auditorium with Casey to pick up her cap and gown. She had been questioned for 7-hours straight by the detectives and it showed all over her face. She walked up behind Aurora and as soon as she got close enough, Sage asked, "What's the problem Simone?" which alerted Aurora and Casey that she was there. The administrator that was charting cap and gown inventory immediately sent for Security. But there was no need. Simone asked her straight out, "Did you try to kill me? Or was it something between Poppy and Chuck? Honestly."

Aurora answered, "My life is too precious to waste on you girl, I don't have no issue with you. I don't know nothing about your cousin, may he rest in peace. All I know is my brother wouldn't kill nobody and he went down South to check out a school down there. It ain't all about you Simone." She had looked Simone right in her eye then turned around to talk with the administrator.

Simone felt she deserved some answers and wanted Aurora to be mature about this, not make a scene because she had an audience. She taps her on the shoulder, "Look, I don't like you, you don't like me. I get it. You gotta know more than *that*. Nobody ain't have no reason to shoot into my door and you're the only one I've ever had a problem with." Simone wasn't going to let it go. "Aurora!" She said sternly. "What is it? Really?" She asked.

"You know what it is, Simone Moncrieff? You always dwell on how you fit into the picture. Even like at Senior Cut Day, I wasn't coming to fight you. I was joining in the festivities. I ain't even see that you had on the Sumo suit until I got to the ring. You got all this stuff in your head and it ain't reality. Like I said, it ain't all about you. Maybe your cousin ain't as squeaky clean as you think. Maybe this ain't got nothing to do with *us*. Yes, I'm sorry that his life has been taken but all I do know is my brother ain't take it and neither did I so...VAMOOSE out my face with this BS!"

Casey started to laugh, "C'mon Rory, she ain't worth it", she said pulling on Aurora. Simone stood thinking about what was said and re-evaluated the layup. It was definitely Chuck. How good of an actress is this girl? She said she would ask her straight up and now she had. She had no choice but to let it go. She received her cap and gown and went on to graduation practice with the other students.

Chapter 7 – "Aurora's Evolution"

It had been 2 years since graduation and Aurora Trotter was finishing up her classes at Mercer County Community College where she earned an Associates Degree in Liberal Arts. Her brother Chuck had been away the entire time and she would visit at least once a month at Annandale to see him. He was now on suicide watch due to a constant string of attempts and his Public Defender was working on his appeal.

Simone Moncrieff's eye witness testimony put Chuck away for 25 years to life. Aurora and her mother and sister had prayed hope upon hope that something would turn around for him. Chuck was at the end of his rope and he couldn't see any other option. His sister felt as if she was doing the time with him. She did well in school and decided to transfer to a 4-year university to further her education.

Aurora was dedicated to her brother's defense and was determined to see him a free man. She never dated, was a dedicated student and worked part-time still at Foot Locker where she had become manager due to Chuck's incarceration.

Their mother Barbara Trotter was working as a Dental Technician in the same office in Ewing and she had aged 10 years due to the ongoing stress of day-to-day struggles and her first born being tried and convicted. She felt all her dreams for him and all she instilled in him was for naught. She was just going through the motions; the spark was gone and she was pretty much living on hope that he would be released on some technicality, praying for him.

Every time she would run into Joyce Moncrieff in a grocery store or at a community affair she would leave. She couldn't bear to look at her. She had seen enough of the Moncrieff family at the trial. She'd even contemplated leaving the city to somewhere more quiet and forgiving. Aurora was raising her sister who was now in the 8th Grade ready to go to the high school in the fall. Connie would come to Aurora for homework help, problems at school, female issues, and the void she felt by the absence of Chuck.

Aurora was doing all she knew to hold the family together and had begun to read the Bible for comfort and stability. She started taking Connie with her to the church on the corner and there she was comforted by the solace that there would be an answer and plan for all of them. She began to pray more often to release some of the guilt she was feeling about her brother's conviction. If she was the reason directly or indirectly, she needed to know that she was forgiven.

Eventually, she came to the place where she knew that forgiveness had to come from Simone first. Would she be given an opportunity? She understood that there were no coincidences; that God works through faith and through people. She waited until she could wait no more. Her next visit to her brother would have to be intense, but as fragile as his state of mind was she would have to be tactful.

On the day she went to see him she went without Connie because she wanted to be direct with him. She never really asked him if he had anything to do with Poppy's death. She just knew her brother. She sat across from him. He looked gaunt and his eyes were sullen like he wasn't getting sleep. She was deeply concerned. "Chuck, how're you? Are you getting enough to eat?" she asked. "I have no appetite. This shit they got in here, man, this ain't no food" he replied with disgust. "What happened, Chuck?" she asked. "That night, what happened with Poppy?"

Chuck pushed his entire face in. "What happened? I wasn't there, that's what the hell happened! I was in the park playing ball. I was the only one there and I shot free throws the whole time. By myself! Why you coming at me with this now?" he asked. "I just never asked you so I…" she was cut off. "Rory, I had nothing to do with Poppy's shooting. They had no prints, no weapon, no nothing!" he said. "And you don't have anybody to verify your alibi, Chuck!" She shot back. He sat up rubbing the top of his head. "Wow, even my own sister don't believe me. How am I supposed to do this alone? Do you understand I'm in here for life? For a murder I didn't do?"

She sat quietly looking at her big brother and that's all it took. She was convinced. "I'm sorry Chuck. There are just so many unanswered questions. I'm in your corner, you know that!" She assured him. Her visit was over.

Aurora's insight into her brother's case piqued her interest into Paralegal Studies. With the inclination alone she began researching the field to see where she could transfer her credits so she could pursue a degree and learn how to apply it to Chuck's case.

She researched the many areas of law and found she would need only a Paralegal Certification to work in the criminal field. She was already over her required credits in Liberal Arts. She knew she was a detail oriented person, had excellent customer service skills from her years at Foot Locker, was extremely organized, possessed the best computer skills of anyone she knew, and her passion and determination guided her to decide to register at Kaplan Online, an 18-month program which will catapult her into the legal field.

T. E. WILLIAMS

Chapter 8 – "No Textbook Answer"

Simone Moncrieff was away at Seminary at Drew Theological School with the intent of continuing in the fall to work on her Bachelor's Degree. She aced her classes and was looking forward to going home to her mother. The long train ride home she thought of Poppy. It had been two years since graduation and she thought of him often but this was different.

She felt pursuing her career as Clergy she would come to understand death and gain some insight spiritually on life, which will ultimately answer the questions she had about death and the afterlife. She was a deep thinker and Simone tended to over think sometimes when it came to the philosophy of any one thing. She knew that about herself. It was first brought to her attention by Aurora Trotter two years ago. She said her name aloud and stared out of the window as each town went by quickly. She took a deep breath, 'maybe I ought to at least give her credit for telling me the truth to my face', she thought. It was something that Aurora, who she didn't see everyday observed about her that people close up never noticed or mentioned. She let out a sigh and thanked the Lord for clarity. There are people who God will put into your life to sharpen you. Not for the hell they put you through, but take something good from it and give them credit. It's iron that sharpens iron, not cotton. Dizzy was cotton. Joyce and Aurora were iron.

The day Joyce decided to hold the latch on her screen door it was not so she could punish Simone, but to help her understand that to be a coward it doesn't take nothing but practice, but to be courageous and face a blizzard, one good time will do. You'll be equipped for the rest of your life.

She decided when the train stopped in Trenton she would go directly to Aurora's home to let her know that; to thank her for saving her years of turmoil by simply telling her the truth.

Exiting the train, Simone Moncrieff evaluated the reasons for her hatred for Aurora Trotter and came to the conclusion that there wasn't one. She rationalized that what she felt wasn't hatred at all. It was just a rebuttal of feelings that she felt were aimed toward her. She also realized on the contrary, that she actually admired her throughout school. Imitation is the sincerest form of flattery.

She summed her and Aurora's relationship up to ongoing issues due to the sharks that swam around them. In a different world, they may have even been allies. She certainly had some likable traits. She didn't know how receptive Aurora would be to this visit but she decided she wasn't going to keep the door closed.

Simone entered her own house on Carroll Street and Joyce her mother had a pot of stew boiling on the stove. The familiar smell brought her back to the night Poppy was murdered and she was feeling nostalgic about it, giggling to herself about the hunk of bread Poppy kept in his cheek still attempting to spoon the meaty stew in as well. The thought then made her laugh out loud and that let Joyce know her baby was home.

"Hey Mony!" She said coming down the stairs to greet her offering hugs and kisses. "Hi Mommy" Simone replied. "It smells so good in here!" Joyce began to get emotional because she hadn't seen Simone in some months and seeing her develop so well gave her a maternal nudge that she'd done a great job with her.

Simone wore a long black trench coat and carried a really good bag and wore classic shoes. She looked lawyerly, professional and she held her head high. Her blonde hair was now cut shorter into a bob and she looked quite educated as a student traveler. She was proud of the accomplishments and adult decisions that Simone made to enhance her life. She didn't take credit, but she knew the stability she provided had a lot to do with it, and she thanked God.

They sat and ate together laughing about Simone's many stories about school and her church, classes and her professors. She talked about how much she was learning about God and her own relationship with Him. Joyce talked about news in the neighborhood and about home in Haiti. Simone was born in Jersey and couldn't identify too much with Haiti, but she had at least been there to understand the landmarks and political climate, the disasters and the level of poverty and distress. She was happy her mother made it here, even if it was through a bad marriage with William. They were young when they married and truly in love. Life just took them in two different directions. At least he provided for Simone and Joyce over the years, and was still financing her education. William remarried and lives in Georgia, but Simone talks to him from time to time.

They talked of Simone's crush on one of her classmates, Todd McClain, which caused Joyce to roar in laughter because she always said Simone was so bossy she could not keep a man. "Too damn mean!" She said, laughing while putting the stew into a storage container. "...And Todd is not a strong enough name to tame my baby! You need a Malachi or a a a an...Adebisi! Todd?" Joyce teased. "You know *Simone* means heard by God?" Simone looks up and says, "Yes, Mommy. You told me all my life. I'm proud to have the strong name you gave me."

"How's your rage, Simone?" Joyce asked looking very serious at her daughter. "I'm okay Mom."

Simone got up to wash the bowls they used for the stew then reached over for the glasses while her mother went in to collect her mail. Simone dropped one of the glasses into the sink and cut her hand. She wrapped a paper towel around the cut which caused quite a bit of blood. "Mom, I cut myself do you have antiseptic?" She hollered to the other room. "Yeah, babe, in the pantry!" Joyce yelled back still separating Simone's mail from her own.

Simone went into the pantry digging through bins where Joyce had organized different whatnots and odds n' ends; threads and string, and crochet items pulling each colored bin forward to view the contents. Then, Simone noticed a weird package wrapped in cellophane, sitting in a red bin on the bottom shelf.

When Simone bent down to pick the package up, she was concerned. It looked like balled up black hair covered in beeswax that had hardened. There was a red rubber band around it. "Mom, what's this?" Simone asked. Joyce continued to separate and had gotten so into the task she began opening her own mail in the process, not really hearing Simone; she happened upon something she hadn't opened at all and became preoccupied with it. Simone brought the package into the kitchen then wrapped the dishtowel tightly around her hand. She again said, "Mom..." but began opening the package with a steak knife. Simone was shocked when she realized what was in the mysterious package and instantly had a flashback...

She's sitting at the table with Poppy talking about the finals they had to take to graduate. She actually hears him say 'I cheated off you', then Detective Hadley is sitting with her on the bench at the Police Station reminding her that Poppy wasn't supposed to be there.

Simone whispers, "He wasn't supposed to be here!" She jumps back, grabs a long roll of paper towels ripping them from the dispenser then wraps up the package and shoves it into her trench coat pocket hanging on the back of a chair. Her mind racing not knowing exactly what to do, she knew that what she shoved into her pocket was drugs...and it was not a dime bag!

"Mommy I got to go, I'll...I'll be back soon!" Simone said throwing her coat on darting out of the door. "Simone?" Joyce said, "Okay Sweetie, don't be long."

Chapter 9 – "Coming Together"

Simone walked her usual brisk thundering march all the way to Southard Street where Aurora lived all her life. She bangs on the door, pacing back and forth, back and forth until Connie opens the door. "I need to see Aurora right now! Is she home?" She said in a panic stricken voice to which Connie replies, "She just pulled up", pointing to the burgundy SUV pulling up to the curb.

Simone thunders down the front steps. "I need to talk to you!" She yelled before Aurora even got out of the car. Aurora notices Simone ranting in front of the windshield with a bloody bandaged hand and picks up her cell phone showing Simone that she intends to call 911, not making any movement in the car and being cautious. She was also watching for Connie to make sure Simone hadn't hurt her.

Then Aurora cracks the window. "What the hell are you doing at my house chick?" Simone realized she looks like a lunatic and calms herself. "Rory, I need to talk to you right now!" She yells, but the expression on her face isn't revealing what Aurora can take a guess at. "What do you want Simone? And what happened to *Vader*?" She says sarcastically. "Look I know it's been two years, but this is about your brother, his freedom!" She yelled. "I need your help!"

Aurora slowly opens the door and gets out. "What's this now?" Aurora asked. "I need to talk to you; only you. Can I please come in? I don't have any weapon; I don't want to hurt anybody. Please."

Aurora jumbled her keys and Simone followed her to her door with her hands out where Aurora can plainly see them. They go into her house where Connie darts off automatically feeling dismissed due to the grown folks' conversation. Aurora did well raising that one. "What about my brother?" She asks.

Simone begins slowly, "The night...Poppy was...killed" she said, out of breath "He wasn't supposed to be at my house. I testified to that in open court, you were there." Aurora responded, "Go on..." Simone begins to pace. "That's it! He wasn't supposed to be there! He was never there on a week night!" Aurora looks at her like she's a giraffe. "So?" Simone stops pacing, her blonde bob seemed to still pace on its own. "He was running from something...somebody! He was hiding!" Aurora, thinking quickly, is trying to understand what Simone is telling her. "So?"

Aurora pulls the package out of her pocket. "This is why he came! I found this, 10 minutes ago in my mother's pantry! I think it's weed or..." Aurora is furious! "You brought drugs in my house with my baby here?" Simone put the package back into her pocket. "Don't you see? He wasn't on a casual visit! He needed to stash this! Somebody was already on to him! It doesn't fit the timeline for your brother to have been in the area! He's innocent Rory!"

Simone flops down on the loveseat. "The night Chuck was on the courts shooting free throws the Defense testified that he was at the courts from around 6:30-7:30pm when he was finally seen by someone at 7:35. So if he was seen at the store at 7:35 by Wilkerson Courts, he couldn't have possibly been at my house on Carroll by 7:40 dressed in all black!"

Aurora was not impressed, "They said that in court chick. They said he could've gotten a ride, or stole a car." Simone reasoned, "Not with the Southard Street Bridge out! There was no way to get to the North Side unless you went through Perry the down town way! Defense didn't even put that in! The alibi works because you can't get over there in 5 minutes without the bridge, plus change into a whole new outfit! The bridge was out almost a year, don't you remember? It covers the time Poppy was killed! Don't you see? He's innocent!"

Aurora stands and begins to pace with her hand over her mouth. "How does this play into it?" She asked pointing to Simone's pocket. "He was shirtless! Nothing but basketball shorts and socks, right? And the New Balances. So how's he gunna get from West Trenton, put on a one piece ninja outfit and knock on my door in 5 minutes with no Southard Street Bridge access, huh? He would have to be Superman. He would have to go through town! You know how Perry Street traffic is!"

"It's impossible!!!" They said in unison.

"Poppy was followed there by someone else; someone who moves a lot like Chuck." Simone said. Aurora said, "Wait, what do you mean moves like him? I thought you saw him in a mask or something." Simone looked awkwardly, "Actually...I uh, identified his layup." She said shyly. "They locked my brother up on the style of a layup? In court you testified that you *saw* him! You didn't see his face? Not even his profile? Oh! No!" Aurora hollered realizing even more. "There's a dude who was booted off the basketball team, Ryan Welling! He moved so much like my brother they called them the Twin Towers! He did Juvy time for possession! We have to do something!"

Aurora and Simone sat thinking about how Defense can introduce new evidence, what to do about the package and how to keep Simone safe, together. If dude learns she knows it wasn't Chuck who did it, her life is in danger as well. They decided to call Detective Hadley and leave a detailed message for Chuck's Public Defender.

"You want some coffee?" Aurora asked. "You got any wine?" Simone asked. They both chuckled. Aurora and Simone were drinking the wine wondering how exactly to approach Detective Hadley with this package when they realized that this was the most they'd ever said to each other.

Chapter 10 – "Growth"

"You know, I was coming over to your house anyway. I wanted to thank you." Simone admitted. "Thank ME? *Vader*?" She jested. "For What?" Simone thought before she answered. "Well the truth is, Rory, nobody ever told me the truth to my face except my mother. That day, in the auditorium, you made me look at myself. You said 'It ain't all about me' and told me that maybe Poppy wasn't as squeaky clean as I thought. I guess he wasn't. I was blind for a long time and I'm sorry. Then I realized I really didn't have anything against you. It was just the crazy people around us who thrived off of it."

"I appreciate that Mony, I really do, and, well, since we're being honest" Aurora stated, "I had gone through a depressive state feeling guilty for what happened to Poppy. I was always talking negatively about you a lot girl; I thought Chuck had heard enough and decided to get rid of you to make my life a little easier. I recently asked him if he had anything at all to do with it. That's how guilty I felt. I was going to ask you to forgive *me*, if something I'd said caused my brother to do it."

Detective Hadley reached the Trotter residence and Aurora opened the door for him. He sat with Simone who was sipping her wine with her legs crossed. "Simone what's going on?" Simone reached into her black trench coat pocket and pulled out the brick. "I found this at my house today. I know for a fact that Poppy stashed it in my mother's pantry the night he died. I came here to the Trotters to let them know Poppy was into some wicked stuff, and he only came over my house as a diversion, but he didn't know he was followed." Simone said pointedly.

"I think I know who killed Poppy." Aurora added, "Ryan Welling. They call him Gap." I didn't put it together all this time because Simone identified my brother in the lineup which I thought was a facial lineup. This dude and my brother, they could be twins from the neck down. And his alibi, the Southard Street Bridge was out. There's no way he could have made it to Simone's house from Wilkerson

Courts in 5 minutes. He was seen by the store clerk at 7:35, which wasn't even mentioned in court. Time of death was confirmed 7:40!"

Detective Hadley took an evidence bag out of his pocket and put the package into it. "You ladies...figured all this out on your own?" Aurora looks over at Simone with a broad smile, "I knew deep down he didn't do it. Plus, Simone and I have never compared notes. Chuck is in a bad way and on suicide watch up at Annandale. We had to work together."

Simone clarifies, "I'm sure Poppy didn't lead him to my house on purpose and I got to thinking about what you said that day. *He wasn't supposed to be there*. I never asked myself, '*why is Poppy here!*' And the question we should be asking now is '*where was Poppy coming from?*' It's not all about me! This package answers that!" Simone informed.

"I remember telling you I didn't have any enemies." Simone said smiling at Aurora "I just want justice to be served for my cousin, even if he wasn't perfect and her brother exonerated.

Detective Hadley couldn't believe his ears. "So you two put your differences to the side to solve this thing? I'm really proud of you girls, very mature. Thank God you called me and not some random uniform cop. Now, we have to ensure Simone's safety and you two are the only ones who are aware that it's this Gap dude right?" The ladies agreed. "Unfortunately we have to house both of you in protective custody." He said with a grin.

"Wha?" Simone looks bewildered. "Huh? Me too?" Aurora hollers. The look on the two of their faces was priceless! "I'm afraid so. You ladies are the reason we're going to get this murderer off the streets of Trenton, and I for one am glad you guys did all the work. Thank you!" He said calling his Department to set up the safe house. "Get some things together." He added with the phone to his ear.

"Well, can I go back home? I got to tell my mom. I don't even have anything here!" Simone asked. "You don't get it do you? Now that you guys have probably been seen together it's not safe. It doesn't take any time to put two and two together. You two just did. This guy killed

Poppy and it's probably gang-related. We already know he's dangerous. Now it's my job to protect and serve. It's your job to listen to me."

"Unbelievable! Simone complained about it throwing her hands in the air and Aurora added "This is insane! I need to hear back from the Public Defender to tell him to add all this to Chuck's appeal file!" Detective Hadley said, "We'll take care of everything."

"C'mon Mony, I have some things you can pack." Aurora said ascending the stairs. The unmarked car picked the two women up driving them to the country to a safe house out of the city. A call was made to Joyce and Barbara to let them know what's going on.

T. E. WILLIAMS

Chapter 11 – "Unlikely Roomies"

Simone Moncrieff paced around the farm house designated as the safe in purple leggings and with her hair tied up in a tangerine bonnet feeling like a caged animal. Aurora was sitting Indian style with her laptop finishing her online homework from Kaplan. "Would you please stop with the pacing chick?" She said. "I'm seriously trying to concentrate over here."

"I don't know, I just feel like we should be doing something." Simone said. "It's only been 4 days Mony." Aurora informed. "We're going to be here for months, maybe a year. You have to find something to occupy your time." Simone looked at the pile of puzzles in the corner. There were adult coloring books, a deck of cards, Pictionary, Jeopardy and an old radio. Simone goes over to the radio turning the dials through static and white noise and finally finds the Gospel station.

"You a Christian Mony?" Aurora asked with no reservations. "Yeah, of course, you're not?" She asked surprised that she had asked. "Nah" Aurora teased, "I worship the Legion of the Undead. They call me *Vader*!" Simone welcomed the jab chuckling. "I can tell! Got me in purple and orange! I look like a Kindergarten class!"

"Don't be talking about my clothes, I got good taste!" Aurora shot back. "I got my own style. I go out of my way not to look like anybody else." Simone couldn't argue there. She walked over to Aurora's closet peeking through her hung clothes. "You do, I'll give you that. You have some really good vintage stuff in here. Where do you shop?" She asked her. Aurora answers without looking up from her laptop. "The thrift store; I've been shopping at the thrift store all my life. First out of necessity, now I choose to. You can find some good stuff. Half the time they don't even know what they have."

Just then a popular song came on that they both knew by Tramaine Hawkins which happen to be appropriate to the conversation and all that had encompassed their relationship entitled *Be Grateful.* The song had always been very special and humbling for Simone. She immediately thought of her mother which prompted her to walk over to the radio to up the volume. She sings softly to the first verse rocking back in forth in the leggings, her arms folded around herself…

> *"God has not promised me sunshine*
>
> *That's not the way it's going to be*
>
> *But a little rain*
>
> *Mixed with God's sunshine*
>
> *A little pain*
>
> *Makes me appreciate the good times"*

Aurora Trotter joins and sings the chorus with her! What an unexpected development! *"Be Grateful!"*

> *"God desires to fill your longings*
>
> *Every pain that you feel*
>
> *He feels them just like you*
>
> *But he can't afford to let you feel only good*
>
> *Then you can appreciate the good times"*

They stand together in the middle of the floor singing and harmonizing dancing around as the tempo of the song picks up. The humble song becomes praise, and praise becomes joy and next thing you know the two were bonding in the Lord!

The pleasing, satisfying song is exactly what they needed to quell the heaviness in the room and put them both at ease. Turns out they had more in common then they ever expected or sought to find. They each had a journey, and as impossible as the moments they spent here were to believe, there they were!

With tears in their eyes they reach over and hug each other releasing years of hate and damage that had been projected onto one another. That's the Spirit of the Lord! He's Holy and Sovereign, and it's what He wants for us. They were delivered, and all the heavy baggage was put down. All the strife, all the weight, all the scars and the guilt was gone in these moments glorifying Him.

"I'm so sorry Rory" Simone cried. "I'm sorry too!" Aurora murmured between tears of deliverance.

They sat up all that night doing each other's hair and talking like they should have been doing in high school. They talked about their respective educational goals, their fears, their celebrity crushes and even talked about the 5th Grade fight. They didn't remember the reason for the fight or why Aurora said she wanted to kick Simone's butt in the first place!

T. E. WILLIAMS

Chapter 12 – "Appeal"

Aurora Trotter was right. It had been months before the appeal for Chuck had been placed on the docket for retrial. His sister had not seen him in months, but his Public Defender gladly kept him updated on the advances that the case made and he made no more attempts to take his own life. He was told that she was in hiding along with the woman who testified against him in the first place. Chuck knew he had someone special in his corner praying for him.

Ryan Welling had been arrested in connection with the murder of Papillion Toussaint and the .38 caliber pistol was found in his home where it was kept unbeknownst to his mother who had been trying to keep him on the straight and narrow since he left the juvenile facility. He had been recruited by a local gang and his job was to kill Poppy in retaliation for the stash that had been taken.

Once ballistics tests were done on the firearm it was matched to the bullet that was extracted from Poppy's body. He pled no contest. When the judge sentenced him, he was given 40 years with no chance of parole. His mother was heartbroken. He stood there dressed so dapper with the teardrop he had earned proudly under his eye crying like somebody should come to save him. It's funny how he could have one grooming lesson and can learn 'yes sir, no sir' so quickly to present himself as a respectable young man in court. If he had only been that way in society instead of trying to move up in an organization that takes lives he would understand how this world really works. He was only 19 years old.

Simone had to testify again. She and Aurora held hands in court until they called her to the stand. She admitted she made a mistake in the identification the first time because of the similarities of their body type and movements. The Defense tried to put her on the spot, but she drew strength from her Lord and made it clear that she was 100% sure it was Gap, who had no alibi for the evening of Poppy's shooting. The jury believed her. Once it was all over Chuck

Trotter's Public Defender did what he had to do to get him released.

Simone and Aurora were both there with their Mothers that day. Chuck walked out of Annandale Prison a free man. Connie ran to him and he takes off running to her hugging them all with everything he had looking over at Simone's family nodding in appreciation. Simone Moncrieff, born in a blizzard as strong as her mother predicted at her birth just walked over to him and said, "I'm so sorry." He grabbed her into the family hug with no words and she whispers, "Glory to God! It was the Christian thing to do."

The End